Megamouse

EMMA LAYBOURN

Andersen Press · London

First published in 2001 by
Andersen Press Limited
20 Vauxhall Bridge Road, London SW1V 2SA
www.andersenpress.co.uk

© 2001 by Emma Laybourn

The right of Emma Laybourn to be identified as the author
of this work has been asserted by her in accordance with
the Copyright, Designs and Patents Act, 1988

British Library Cataloguing in Publication Data available
ISBN 1 84270 013 8

Phototypeset by Intype London Ltd
Printed and bound in Great Britain by the
Guernsey Printing Company Limited, Guernsey,
Channel Islands

1

'Go on,' said Kelly. 'I dare you! Your granpa'll never know.'

Joe shook his head unhappily. 'I can't.'

'Of course you can! Don't be so soft! It's *your* living room!'

'Not any more,' said Joe gloomily. 'It's Granpa's room now.'

'So? It's still your house! If your granpa doesn't want anyone to use his computer, he should lock his door. But he hasn't, has he?'

Joe shook his head. His fingers curled around the door-handle.

He told himself there was nothing to be afraid of. Granpa was at the University, where he was probably growling at terrified students right now. He wouldn't be home till Dad fetched him; and Dad was out at work, too, painting somebody's kitchen. Mum was busy upstairs feeding baby Rose. It was the perfect opportunity. But all the same . . .

'If this was *my* house, I wouldn't think twice,' said Kelly. 'Go on, Joe! *Please*! I've got all these brilliant games, and our computer's too old to run them!'

She hopped impatiently up and down, waiting for Joe's answer. He gave in.

'All right . . . Just for a bit.'

'Good for you! *Martian Warlord* first!'

Joe pushed open the door.

The living room felt strange. It felt *alien*. Dad had only just finished decorating it, and fitting new patio doors, when Granpa broke his leg and had to move in. It had been Granpa's room ever since.

Joe was left with nowhere to spread out his race track. There were no more cosy evenings snuggling in front of the TV – he had to watch TV perched on a hard chair in the kitchen. The room didn't feel like part of his home any more. It had been taken over by Granpa's things – his bed, his bookshelves, and especially the computer that sat big and square on Granpa's desk.

It was a gleaming, new and very expensive computer. Around it teetered piles of computer disks, boxes full of computer bits, and snaking coils of tangled wire. In the middle of the wire maze sat a packet of digestive biscuits and a large square cage, where a white rat crouched glaring at them.

'A *rat*? What's your granpa doing with a *rat*?' whispered Kelly.

'Don't ask me. She's called Cleo. She doesn't like me.'

'Cleo! Cleo!' Kelly tapped softly on the bars. The

white rat turned its back on her and began to clean its whiskers.

'I wish I had a pet,' said Kelly wistfully. 'Even a rat would be better than nothing.'

Joe was getting twitchy. 'Come on! If you don't want to play, let's go!'

'Of course I want to play!' Kelly pulled the *Martian Warlord* disk from her pocket. Then she looked round, puzzled.

'Bother! Where's the mouse?' she complained. 'There's a rat – but no mouse!'

'Maybe we should just leave it . . . '

But Kelly was rummaging through the piles of equipment on the desk. 'Aha! Here we are!' she said triumphantly. 'This'll do. Must be new – it's still in its box.' She read aloud from the label.

'MEGAMOUSE
ADVANCED COMPUTER MOUSE
WITH MEMORY, BACK-UP BATTERIES
AND OPTIC CELLS – what are they?'

'Like eyes, I think,' said Joe, 'but – '

'AND OPTIC CELLS FOR FASTER DOCU-MENT READING,' finished Kelly. She tipped the mouse out on to the mouse mat. Carefully, Joe set it upright. Its grey plastic dome was cool and smooth to the touch.

'If it's new, we probably shouldn't use it,' he said anxiously.

'What's the problem? A mouse is a mouse. They're all the same. Give it here!'

THUMP! Something heavy crashed into the patio door, making Joe jump in alarm.

'*What's that*?'

A wrinkled black nose was squashed against the glass. A pair of watery, bad-tempered eyes glowered at him.

'It's only that awful bulldog from next door,' said Kelly, who lived next door but one. She plugged the mouse's cable into the computer. 'It belongs to that woman who moved in last week. She calls it Hogarth. Horrible Hogarth. Just ignore it! Relax, Joe! You're as jumpy as a flea!'

Joe turned away from the snarling face at the window, as Kelly loaded up the game.

'Be careful,' he pleaded.

'I'm *being* careful! Watch out, Martian Warlord. Here come Jumpin' Joe and Killer Kelly!'

She was Killer Kelly all right. Joe had to admit it – she was a whiz at computer games. Joe was hopeless. He always seemed to end up dead.

'These Martians are really wicked!' said Kelly, her fingers busy. 'The blue ones are the best. They've got nine tentacles and they'll slime you with poisonous goo if you don't zap them!'

Kelly was good at zapping them. Martians

exploded in slimy splurts all over the screen. Their spaceships turned into golden fireballs. Kelly was *quick*.

Much quicker than me, thought Joe. I can't do that! He was all thumbs on the computer. They'd never had one before Granpa arrived: and he'd only used this one twice, with Granpa frowning over his shoulder and going 'Hrmph!' under his breath. It hadn't been much fun.

The bulldog thudded on the glass again, squinting hungrily at Cleo's cage. The white rat ignored it.

'Bother that dog!' exclaimed Kelly. 'Now I've gone and got myself killed, and I'm only on level three! Your turn, Joe.'

She darted at the window, waving her arms and pulling faces. The bulldog backed away.

Joe slid into her seat. He held the mouse tightly, clicking its buttons, and fixed his eyes on the Martian Invaders, as they belched blue slime and slashed out with their plasma swords.

But he couldn't concentrate. He kept thinking he heard the car outside, and his heart would pound and his fingers stop. And then he got drenched in blue slime.

It wasn't fair. Granpa had taken over the house. Granpas were supposed to be kind old men who gave you toffees, thought Joe resentfully, not snappy old tyrants who barked out orders and gave you maths tests that you didn't want and kept on asking if you'd left your brains in bed . . .

Joe winced at the memory, and his hand clenched on the mouse. Angrily he clicked its buttons in a rapid tattoo, not caring about what part of the screen he was clicking on.

'Gotcha! Gotcha!' he muttered. But it was Granpa he was zapping, not the Martians.

'What are you *doing*?' said Kelly. 'That's not how you play!'

There was a dazzling flash. Then the screen went blank.

Beneath Joe's hand, the mouse quivered. It shot away from him across the desk, and tumbled onto the floor.

2

'What on earth are you playing at?' hissed Kelly.

'Nothing!' said Joe, bewildered.

'You tell *me* to be careful, and then *you* go and throw the mouse on the floor!'

'But I didn't throw it! It jumped!'

'Oh, sure,' snorted Kelly, stooping to pick up the mouse.

The instant she touched it, it darted away. It shot under the desk and disappeared behind a box of paper. Only its tail, a long grey cable, could be seen sticking out.

Kelly recoiled, banging her head on the desk. 'What's going on?'

'It came alive,' Joe whispered.

'Rubbish! It can't have!' Kelly began to scrabble under the desk, but Joe pulled her back.

'Wait! Let me!' Kneeling down, he cautiously reached behind the paper box until he felt something cool and smooth and rounded. It quivered at his touch.

Joe held the mouse gently, until it was still. Then, wrapping his fingers carefully round it, he lifted it up.

7

'*Batteries*!' said Kelly. 'Of course! It's got batteries. *That's* how it moved.' She sounded relieved.

Joe cupped the Megamouse in his hand. He felt almost afraid of hurting it, as if it were a flesh and blood mouse, not plastic. He put it gently on the desk.

'It came alive,' he murmured.

Kelly picked up the mouse and jiggled it. 'Doesn't feel alive to me.' She plonked it back on the mouse mat, where it sat like a lump of stone. 'Doesn't look alive either,' she said. 'Let's plug it in again. I hope it still works, after being thrown around like that!'

She switched off the computer, reconnected the mouse, and powered it back up. The screen flickered, and a single word flashed out. But it wasn't READY. It wasn't even ERROR. It was:

'GREETING.'

'That's not right!' said Kelly.

Joe gaped at the screen. Then, reaching past Kelly, he hesitantly typed:

'WHO ARE YOU?'

'MEGAMOUSE,' said the screen.

Joe stared down at the mouse. He put his hand gently on it, and felt it tremble.

'GREETING, LIGHT HAND,' said the screen.

'*What*?' exclaimed Kelly.

Joe looked down at his hands. 'I think it means me,' he said. He typed in:

'I AM CALLED JOE.'

8

'GREETING, CALLED JOE.'

'NO, JUST JOE.'

'GREETING, JUST JOE.'

Joe gave up. 'CALL ME LIGHT HAND.'

'I've heard about programs like this,' said Kelly. 'You can program a computer to have a conversation just like a real person . . . You wouldn't mistake this one for a real person, though! Nobody talks like that!'

'HOW DO YOU DO?' typed Joe.

'HOW DO I DO WHAT?'

'HOW ARE YOU?'

'HOW AM I WHAT?'

Kelly giggled. 'Weird program!'

'It's not a program. It's alive,' said Joe firmly.

'Then why is it talking in such a funny way?'

'I'm asking the wrong sort of questions,' said Joe. He thought carefully, and typed in:

'HOW ARE YOU MADE?'

This time the reply came readily.

'92% MOULDED POLYCARBONATE PLASTIC, RECHARGEABLE 15 VOLT BATTERY, 18 MEGABYTES OF MEMORY. HOW MANY MEGABYTES DO YOU HAVE?'

Joe scratched his head. 'I don't know!'

'It can't be alive, Joe,' said Kelly. 'It's just programmed to say things. It's good though, isn't it? I bet it's –'

Kelly stopped in mid-sentence. The two children

9

stared at each other as, outside, a car engine coughed to a halt. Car doors clunked, twice.

'*Granpa*!'

Joe heard the smack of crutches on the path, and turned pale.

'Quick! Before he finds us!'

Swiftly, Kelly shut down the computer. Joe snatched up the Megamouse and put it back in its box. They heard the front door open.

'Out the back!' They scrambled for the patio door and slipped out into the back garden, just as Grandpa entered the hall.

Joe and Kelly crept round to the kitchen, hoping to sneak in until they heard Granpa's imperious voice through the window.

'I'll have a chop for my tea,' he was saying. 'Peas, *not* carrots.'

'Yes, Gerald,' said Mum's voice in reply.

'And apple sauce. Smooth, *not* lumpy.'

'All right, Gerald.'

Kelly pulled a face at Joe.

'Bossy, isn't he?' she whispered.

'I have some very important work to do this evening,' Granpa went on, 'so I want tea as soon as possible. I'll have a coffee now. Three sugars.' His crutches clattered to the floor as he sat down.

'Wow! What an old grump. I'm glad he's not *my* granpa!' whispered Kelly.

'Come in with me,' urged Joe.

'No way!' Kelly shook her head. 'Sorry, Joe. I'm off home.'

Joe slunk inside, hoping Granpa wouldn't notice him.

'So, what have you been up to, young fella?' asked Granpa sharply.

'Playing in the garden with Kelly,' muttered Joe. He was sure Granpa suspected something. Luckily Rose began to wail, and Joe busied himself with bouncing her on his lap until she giggled. Her wriggly, wobbly legs kicked against his own. Her starfish fingers pulled at the tablecloth and slopped Granpa's cup of tea.

'Careful!' said Granpa sharply. Rose gazed up at Granpa's frown and her face crinkled into wails again.

'I hope she's not going to keep that up all evening,' said Granpa. 'I need peace and quiet! I can't work with that racket.'

'She's only three months old,' said Mum mildly. 'I'll try and keep her quiet, but babies still cry a lot at that age.'

'I like a bit of noise while *I'm* working,' said Dad cheerfully. 'Don't like things too quiet.'

'Painting window-frames doesn't exactly tax the brain, though, does it?' snapped Granpa. 'It's not what I expected a son of mine to end up doing.'

'It's what I'm good at,' said Dad. He drained his tea and walked out of the kitchen.

Joe felt like snapping right back at Granpa. How dare he talk to Dad that way, when he was living in Dad's house! Only it seemed to be Granpa's house now. Everything revolved around Granpa.

Joe didn't dare say anything, though. He felt guilty about using Granpa's computer. He kept his head down as he helped Mum make the tea. It was mashed potato again . . . they seemed to have mash all the time now, because Granpa liked it. Joe didn't.

Halfway through tea, he stopped eating.

'What's the matter, Joe?' asked Mum.

'Nothing.' But the mash had just turned to cotton wool in his mouth. He could hardly swallow for the fear that had gripped him.

He hadn't closed the patio door properly. He was sure of it! He'd left it open a crack. As soon as Granpa went into his room, he'd see it, and then Granpa would *know* . . .

3

Megamouse sat on his mouse mat, and wondered.

What was he? Where was he? He'd been awoken by a chance command that he couldn't now remember. Before that, there was nothing. After that, everything.

Who had woken him? A small, light hand had held him gently. But now Light Hand had gone.

Megamouse had no ears, yet he could hear. Sounds vibrated through his delicate circuits. And, with his optic cells, he could also see. Now he saw that he was not alone.

In the cage nearby, there was a scurry of activity. The white rat was busily clawing at the catch on her door, until it fell open with a click. She slipped out, scampered across the desk, and helped herself to a digestive biscuit from the open packet.

Cleo dragged the biscuit over to Megamouse. Sitting up on her thin haunches, she stared at him bright-eyed. Then she began to squeak.

Megamouse listened. He analysed the squeaks. It only took him a few milliseconds; Rat was not very difficult. He soon translated Cleo's squeaks as:

'Do you want some biscuit?'

She dropped a piece in front of him.

Megamouse tipped his box over and rolled out to survey the biscuit. What was he supposed to do with it? He had no mouth. He tried rolling over it, but that just turned it into crumbs.

As he moved, his little wheel squeaked faintly. This gave Megamouse an idea. He practised rolling and squeaking until he got his answer right.

'No eat,' he squeaked.

Although it wasn't very good Rat, Cleo understood.

'You don't eat!' she exclaimed. 'Then what do you live on?'

'Desk.'

'No, no! I mean food! You are a mouse, aren't you? They *called* you a mouse.' Cleo studied him doubtfully.

'Me Megamouse!'

'Not much of a mouse, if you ask me,' sniffed Cleo. 'Where's your fur? Where's your whiskers, and your tail?'

'Me got tail,' squeaked Megamouse hopefully, waving his cable.

'Hmph,' snorted Cleo. 'Funny sort of tail. Oh, well. If you're staying, I'd better show you round my room. Come on!'

Gracefully she leapt down to the chair, and then to the floor.

'Bye-bye up!' squealed Megamouse, throwing

himself recklessly after her. He tumbled onto the carpet, unhurt.

'Nice big mouse mat,' he said approvingly.

'Pay attention! Now, this is the fire.'

'Fire,' repeated Megamouse.

'When it's orange and hisses, don't go near it! It bites. This is the bin, good for apple cores. Just here under the bed, I've made a nice little nest of tissues. You can share it if you want,' said Cleo.

'Me like nests?'

'All mice like nests.'

Megamouse rolled under the bed and rummaged in the tissues. Shreds of paper caught annoyingly in his wheel.

'Me not like nests,' he declared.

'Hmph,' said Cleo. 'Some mouse. Anyway, see that hole in the skirting board? That's the way out. It goes right through to the garden. I don't think the humans know about it. Handy if you fancy an earwig or want to play outside.'

'Outside?'

Cleo pointed her nose at the window. 'Out there.'

Megamouse stared. Like a huge computer screen, the window was full of shapes and colours, shifting, changing . . .

'Nice game,' he said. 'Big big game! Me want play Outside!'

'I'll take you later on,' promised Cleo. 'Now, here's the stick I keep for gnawing. Granpa doesn't

15

like the wires being chewed, so if you want to keep your teeth down...' She peered closely at him. 'Have you *got* any teeth?'

'No teeth,' squeaked Megamouse. 'No mouth. No eat.' Yet he felt suddenly hungry. Something was calling him, singing enticingly... something he needed...

Mesmerised, he followed the song. It led straight under the bed, to the wall – to an electric power socket.

'Hungry,' sighed Megamouse. Without hesitation, he twitched his wire tail around, inserted it into the socket and –

'Hey!' shrieked Cleo in horror. 'Stop! You'll fry!'

But Megamouse didn't budge. He felt electricity race through his wires, blaze along his circuits, and fill his batteries brimful. Cleo's whisker sizzled when it brushed against him, and she pulled away in alarm.

'Stop it!' she squealed. 'You'll frizzle up like a rasher of burnt bacon!'

'Food,' said Megamouse happily, pulling out his tail. 'Yum, yum.' He felt bouncing with energy, as the current rocketed round his metal veins.

Cleo was trembling. 'Don't you *dare* do that again!'

But Megamouse ignored her. Peering out from under the bed, he gazed at the patio door.

'Someone playing Outside,' he announced.

'What?' As Cleo turned to look, the patio door was nudged open. A squat figure with watery eyes shouldered its way through, and waddled into the room on four short, bandy legs.

'Quick,' said Cleo. 'Get back on the desk!'

'Me no climb!'

The bulldog stood in the middle of the room, his breath noisy and rasping, his hungry gaze fixed on Cleo.

'Stay under the bed! Don't move!' Cleo hissed to Megamouse. She leapt at the quilt, and raced up it to the bed, hoping to get to safety and distract Hogarth's attention from Megamouse at the same time.

From the bed, it was only a short leap to the desk – but Hogarth was after her. Huffing and puffing, he scrabbled onto Granpa's bed, his claws ripping at the quilt. He jumped clumsily across to the desk, and only just made it. As he clattered over the keyboard after the white rat, piles of disks slithered to the floor.

Cleo jumped away from him to land lightly on the edge of the bin. Leaping after her, the bulldog thudded into the bin, which tipped over and sent him rolling across the floor in a shower of pencil shavings.

He staggered to his feet, growling at Cleo. But before he could pounce, a small, grey object shot

17

across the carpet, clicking wildly, and stopped by his feet. Hogarth sniffed it curiously.

'Ruff!' he snorted, and opened his jaws to bite. All at once, a white, furry missile launched itself at his other end.

'Megamouse – hide!' squealed Cleo, as her teeth met in Hogarth's tail. Hogarth yelped and flung himself against the desk. A landslide of paper slid down over him. Galloping around the room, Hogarth tried to shake off the terrible pain in his tail.

Footsteps thudded down the hall. Cleo let go and hurtled like a white bullet back up the bed to the desk. Hogarth blundered to the patio door and charged out into the garden.

The door from the hall was flung open. There was a long silence while Granpa, leaning on his crutches, took in the upturned bin, the snowdrifts of papers and scattered disks. Cleo sat innocently in her cage with her head on one side.

Granpa took a deep breath.

'Joe!' he bellowed. 'Come in here *this minute!*'

4

'It wasn't me!' Joe protested, staring at the mess. But even as he spoke, he felt himself flushing guiltily.

'Have you been in here, Joe?' asked Dad quietly.

'Well?' thundered Granpa. 'Yes or no?'

'Only for a bit,' Joe mumbled.

'What for?' asked Dad. 'I thought you were outside. You know this is Granpa's room.'

Joe glared at him. Dad should be sticking up for him! He should tell Granpa this was *their* room, and they could go in it when they liked!

'I was playing *Martian Warlord*,' he muttered. 'It's a game of Kelly's.'

'You've been using my computer?' Granpa's brows gathered together darkly. 'Just look at the mess you've made! Papers everywhere – *and what's this mouse doing on the floor*?' He bent down stiffly and picked up Megamouse from the carpet.

'I don't know,' said Joe miserably.

'It's a brand new piece of equipment!' snapped Granpa. 'Hasn't even been tested yet!'

'But I put it back in its box!' protested Joe.

'Ah! So you *did* use it!'

19

'It was the only mouse we could see,' said Joe.

'And why is it on the floor? I suppose it jumped out and ran around all by itself?'

'It must have!' Joe blurted out. 'It came alive while we were playing and ran off, and it talked to us on the screen and called me Light Hand . . .'

He knew at once it was the wrong thing to say. His voice trailed away. Granpa was staring at him as if he was mad.

'Nice story, son,' said Dad sympathetically. 'But what really happened? Did Kelly make this mess?'

'No! Neither of us!'

'Then who did?' Granpa's voice was as cold as ice.

Joe swallowed. He didn't know what to say.

'May I come in?'

They all turned. A young woman lolled against the patio door. Without waiting for an answer, she stepped over the threshold and tossed back a shock of gleaming hair.

'I'm your new neighbour, Prunella Tree,' she said. Her eyes twinkled as she smiled ruefully. 'Oh, dear! What a terrible mess that dreadful dog of mine has made! I came straight round to apologise.'

Granpa let out his breath with a snort like a surfacing whale.

'Your dog?'

'Wicked Hogarth!' said Miss Tree. 'He keeps finding a way through the fence. But don't worry.

It won't happen again!' Her smile flashed out brilliantly. 'Do let me tidy up this dreadful mess for you!'

'No need,' said Granpa, looking a little dazed. But Prunella Tree was already on her knees, picking up Granpa's disks and papers. She set them down by the computer, and then clapped her hands together with a gasp of delight.

'Oh! I don't believe it! You've got a XF900! Now that is a computer I would love to own. So fast! So powerful!'

'I helped develop it,' said Granpa, looking rather pleased.

'No! Really?' Miss Tree was rapt. 'And the processor – the PDQ? Did you develop that as well?'

'I had a hand in that,' said Granpa. He actually *smiled*. Joe was astounded. He couldn't remember ever seeing Granpa smile. 'It won an award, you know.'

'I know! It's famous! I'm in computers too, just in a small way, writing games – nothing like you! The creator of the PDQ! And to think my dog's been sticking his muddy paws all over it!' Miss Tree shook her head. 'Naughty Hogarth.'

'My grandson blamed the mouse,' said Granpa. He chuckled. 'Told me it came alive and ran around the room!'

'What a sweet idea,' said Prunella Tree. Idly, she picked up Megamouse.

'Stop!' cried Joe. Everyone stared at him. 'I mean

21

– stop tidying up,' he stammered. 'I should be doing that. I left the door open, so it was my fault Hogarth got in.'

'Glad to hear you admit it,' grunted Granpa, as Joe took the Megamouse from Miss Tree's hand and put it carefully back in its box. He couldn't feel a twitch of movement . . . but he knew it *had* come alive.

He began to pick up the rest of Granpa's things, while Dad helped.

'I'm glad it wasn't you,' whispered Dad, winking at him. 'But no more silly stories as excuses, eh?'

Miss Tree lingered, talking to Granpa about bytes and bits and bandwidths. Joe wished she'd go away. He was glad when she ran a casual finger along the bars of Cleo's cage, and Cleo tried to nip her.

'I can see Hogarth outside,' he said. 'I think he's digging up the garden.'

'Dreadful dog! He's supposed to be company for me, but he's a complete idiot,' sighed Miss Tree as she strolled to the door.

'I know the feeling,' said Granpa. 'Come back some time! It's nice to have an intelligent conversation. Come round for a cup of tea!'

'I will! I will!' she promised, and was gone.

'It's not even his house,' said Joe, 'and he invited her round as if he owned the place.'

'I don't mind,' said Mum. 'Are you drying?'

'Granpa likes Miss Tree better than me,' said Joe.

Mum handed him a dripping plate. Rose sat in her bouncing chair and gurgled at them.

'Granpa's not used to small boys,' said Mum. 'He's never got to know you properly.'

'Never tried,' muttered Joe. There had never been outings to the park or the zoo with Granpa. Granny, yes; but Granpa had always been too busy. 'He doesn't even like Rose!'

'He's not used to babies either.'

'Does Granpa *have* to stay with us?'

'Well, yes, he does, until his leg's better!' said Mum.

'How long will that take?' Joe asked.

'It could be a few months, at his age.'

'Oh, no!' wailed Joe. Baby Rose began to wail too. Mum picked her up and cuddled her.

'He can't manage by himself,' she said. 'If he wasn't here, he might have to live in a nursing home. He wouldn't be able to work. His work's very important, you know.'

'I know,' growled Joe. 'He keeps telling us.'

'He should have retired by now, but the University keeps asking him back. He's a very clever man, your granpa.'

'Thinks he's Brain of Britain,' muttered Joe. 'I'm not surprised Granny divorced him.' He said it under his breath, so that Mum wouldn't hear. She'd only tell him off.

23

He couldn't understand why Mum was so patient with Granpa, when Granpa was so rude to *her*. Just because Dad was only a painter and decorator, and Mum used to work in a shop . . .

Mum gave him a hug with her free arm. He breathed in Rose's milky scent.

'I know he's grumpy sometimes,' said Mum, 'but remember he's a long way from home, and his leg hurts. And I think he's lonely.'

'Lonely? How can he be lonely?'

'Well, we can't talk to him about the things he cares about,' said Mum. 'Maybe this Prunella Tree will be good for him. She sounds like a nice lady. *You* try and be nice to him, too.'

'Mmm,' said Joe. Mum ruffled his hair.

'How about a board game once Rose is asleep?' she asked. 'You can choose.'

Granpa's voice bellowed from his study.

'Newspaper! Where's the newspaper?'

Rose began to cry. Mum picked her up, along with the paper, and carried them both out.

Joe clattered the plates angrily.

'He thinks we're all his servants,' he said to the fridge. 'He thinks we're all stupid. But I know something he doesn't! Megamouse *did* come alive! I'm not making it up! I'll prove it – somehow!'

5

'Want to go on the computer, hey?'

Joe looked up from his book in surprise. There stood Granpa, leaning on his crutches, his tall, bent frame filling the doorway. His eyebrows bristled alarmingly.

'Well? What do you say? Lost your tongue?'

'No – I mean, yes – yes, please!' stammered Joe.

'Come on, then!'

Joe followed Granpa into his room. Cleo ran to and fro on the desk, jumping nimbly over wires. Granpa stroked her with a crooked finger, and Joe felt bold enough to ask:

'Where did you get Cleo, Granpa?'

'University,' grunted Granpa. 'She was a lab rat.'

It took Joe a minute to work out what he meant. 'You mean they were going to do experiments on her?'

'Might have.'

Joe stared at Granpa. Rescuing rats didn't sound like the Granpa he knew.

'Boys like games,' said Granpa. 'Don't they? Hey?'

'Yes,' said Joe. 'Usually.'

'Got some computer games for you to play.'

'Really? Oh! Granpa – thanks!'

Granpa started up the computer. A mouse sat ready on the mouse mat, but not the mouse Joe was hoping for. Glancing up, he spotted Megamouse hunched in a box on a shelf out of reach. He wanted to ask Granpa about it; but that might spoil Granpa's good mood.

'You see if you can find the games file,' said Granpa. Joe saw his old, gnarled hand sneak over to stroke Cleo's ears.

He's being quite nice! thought Joe, as he clicked on the mouse.

'What are you doing?' snapped Granpa, grabbing the mouse back. 'Not that file!'

Nice to rats, anyway, thought Joe. Oh, well.

'Here we are,' announced Granpa. 'Here's your first game. Maths Hound. Help you do better at school.'

On to the screen waddled a sad-eyed spotty dog. 'IF YOU GET THE SUM RIGHT, I GET A BONE!' it told Joe. 'I HOPE YOU'RE RIGHT, BECAUSE I'M HUNGRY! HERE'S YOUR FIRST SUM. $2413 \div 127 = ?$'

Joe gulped. 'I can't do that!'

'Hrmph!' Granpa raised an eyebrow. 'All right. Let's try an easier one.'

'47 x 13?' asked Maths Hound mournfully. '18 x 9?'

'I need a pencil and paper,' said Joe desperately. Even the easiest sums were suddenly too hard, with Granpa snorting at his shoulder. He couldn't think straight. He guessed wildly, and got nearly all the sums wrong, while Maths Hound wept and howled.

'Hrmph! Thought you'd do better than that,' sniffed Granpa. 'Let's try the other game. Here we are! Spelling Bee.'

A fat yellow bee flitted across the screen.

'Let's spell *enthusiastic*!' buzzed the speaker.

Joe nearly groaned aloud. He was hopeless at spelling.

Game? he thought. This isn't a game – it's a form of torture!

His stomach began to hurt, and his sweating fingers slipped on the keyboard.

'WRONG!' buzzed the bee. Joe felt hot and ashamed. All the spellings he knew drained out of his head. He couldn't spell MISERABLE. He couldn't spell TRIAL. He couldn't even spell CABBAGE.

'Hrmph!' said Granpa at last. 'Think you need to practise.'

'I'm usually better than that at spelling,' pleaded Joe. 'It's just harder on a computer.'

Granpa looked sceptical. 'Maybe so.' He cleared his throat. 'Well, Joe, I've decided you can practise on this computer if you want, while I'm at work. Just Maths Hound and Spelling Bee, mind. And ask your mother first. And don't leave the patio door open. Well? Aren't you pleased?'

'Yes. Oh, yes. Thanks, Granpa,' said Joe dismally.

He escaped upstairs and slumped, exhausted, on his bed. Unspellable words floated before his eyes; unsolvable sums rattled hollowly in his brain.

I'm going to have nightmares about bees and hounds, he thought. The idea of playing Granpa's games again filled him with dread.

'I'll just lose,' he said. 'It'll be awful. I don't want to do sums – I want to play with Megamouse!'

Then a thought struck him. He had permission to use the computer. Why shouldn't he play with Megamouse? Granpa hadn't told him not to. Anyway, Granpa wouldn't be there. Granpa wouldn't know.

6

'Go on!' said Joe. 'Please, Kelly.'

All day at school he'd thought of nothing but Megamouse: of plugging him in and talking to him again. But he was afraid of doing something wrong. He wanted Kelly's help.

'No thanks!' said Kelly. 'Not if it just means playing those stupid maths and spelling games. They sound awful.' She swung her school bag over her shoulder, and kicked a can along the pavement.

'I bet you'd be good at them,' said Joe. 'And you could bring *Martian Warlord*, and your other games.'

Kelly looked at him suspiciously. 'I thought you weren't allowed to play those?'

'But Granpa won't know! Go on, Kelly, please! I'll give you half my chocolate.' Joe held out the bar he'd just bought, on the way home from school.

'All of it,' said Kelly.

'Done!'

A silver jeep pulled up alongside them, and the window glided open.

'Like a lift, children?' Miss Tree pushed up her sunglasses and gave them an encouraging grin.

29

'No thanks,' said Joe coldly.

But Kelly said, 'Nice car!'

'Isn't it?' agreed Miss Tree. 'There's good money in computer games. Perhaps you two could help me write my next one?'

'Would we get paid? How much do you get?' asked Kelly eagerly.

'Oh, enough for the car, a boat, a country cottage . . . I've just been over to my cottage in Acrefield. You must come there one day and bring your granpa, Joe. It's a funny old place, full of mice . . . How's that little mouse of yours?'

'What mouse?' Startled, Joe tried to look blank.

'The computer mouse that came alive.' Miss Tree's eyes sparkled with amusement.

'Oh, that! I'd forgotten all about that,' lied Joe. 'It was just – it was just a joke.'

'It didn't come alive,' explained Kelly. 'It just had a really odd program.'

'Well, do let me know if it happens again! I'd love to see a computer mouse that could run around on its own!'

Joe began to walk on determinedly. The silver jeep glided past them.

'I wouldn't have minded a lift,' said Kelly. 'Do you think she meant it about the games?'

'She was showing off,' said Joe.

'Nice car, though,' said Kelly wistfully.

By the time they trudged up the hill to Kelly's

house, the jeep was parked in its drive, and Miss Tree was striding down the pavement with Hogarth on a lead.

'Look,' said Kelly. 'She's taking Hogarth for a drag. Poor thing! She's choking him!'

'I thought you said Hogarth was horrible?'

'He's not *that* horrible,' said Kelly. 'Hang on, while I get my games – we should have an hour before your granpa gets home!'

Joe felt guilty as they sneaked into Granpa's room. The guilt lasted just as long as it took to switch on the computer. Joe took down Megamouse's box, and plugged the mouse in.

'HALLO, MEGAMOUSE.'

He received an instant reply.

'GREETING, LIGHT HAND.'

'He knows you!' whispered Kelly.

'HOW ARE YOU GOING?' asked Joe.

'ON MY LITTLE WHEEL.'

'Let me!' said Kelly. Grabbing Megamouse, she typed:

'HI, MEGAMOUSE!'

'GREETING, FAST HAND.'

'He knows me too!' said Kelly in delight. 'He's cute! I wish I could take him home.'

'He's not a pet,' said Joe. He glanced around the room. He had the oddest feeling that they were being watched, even though there was nobody there with them but Cleo – and she was busy burrowing

31

in her straw. He looked hard at the windows. Nothing. But he felt uneasy.

'I'd better put Spelling Bee on, just in case,' he said. He had an awful feeling Granpa was going to walk in.

'SPELLING BEE,' he requested.

'GAME GOOD LIKE GAME!'

'I wish I did,' said Joe, as he started to play.

This time, to his amazement, he was good at it. Not just good – he was terrific! He got every spelling right, even though he'd never heard of some of the words before. They just seemed to spell themselves!

'I don't believe this,' breathed Joe. Soon he was on the top level, and the bee was telling him he was a genius.

'I thought you were no good at this?' asked Kelly.

'It's not me doing it! It's Megamouse!'

'EASY!' said Megamouse. 'HARD GAME, PLEASE.'

'Let's try Maths Hound.' The mournful spotty dog appeared on the screen.

'256 x 78 = ?' it asked.

Quick as lightning, the answer appeared: '19968.' Maths Hound's tail wagged furiously, as he was awarded a bone.

Joe was astounded. The answers seemed to fill themselves in before he'd even read the questions.

'HARDER SUMS, PLEASE!' said Megamouse. Kelly took over. Before long, Maths Hound had disappeared under a pile of bones, and the children had top score in the Hall of Fame.

Joe grinned. 'Just wait till Granpa sees that!'

'EASY EASY!' said Megamouse. 'MORE GAMES, PLEASE. I LIKE PLAYING GAMES.'

Joe laughed. 'SO DO I – WITH YOU!'

'Let's try *Martian Warlord*!' suggested Kelly.

Joe started up *Martian Warlord*. At once, Megamouse's buttons began to click. Then he was off, racing across the mouse mat so fast that it was all Joe could do to keep his hand on him.

On the screen, Joe's spaceship became a blur. Somehow it avoided every enemy laser. It zapped so many Martian ships that fireballs littered the screen. It was the most enchanting hour of Joe's life. His score climbed to level after level, while beside him Kelly yelped with excitement.

'Yes!' she cried, punching the air. She covered her mouth in mock alarm. 'Sorry! But level twenty! That's incredible!'

Joe's score appeared on the screen.

'LIGHT HAND 80,000 points.'

'It should say Megamouse,' said Joe. 'It's *him* doing it.'

'Let me try *Viking Raiders*!' begged Kelly. 'That's a real stinker. I've never managed to finish it!'

Joe let her take over. Soon she'd killed all the

Vikings, stolen their treasure and had a record score.

'QUICK HAND 92,000,' said the screen. 'EASY! WHAT SHALL WE PLAY NOW? HARD GAME, PLEASE.'

'Got any more?' asked Joe.

'PLAY OUTSIDE?' suggested Megamouse.

'Outside? I don't know that one.' Kelly fished in her bag for another CD. 'Here's *Roadhog Racers*. It's the most difficult one I've got.'

Roadhog Racers was a walkover for Megamouse. He beat every other car on the track by miles, and never crashed once.

'EASY EASY EASY!' he announced.

'Tea-time!' called Mum. She stuck her head round the door, and Joe hastily leant across the computer screen.

'You two have spent long enough on that machine now,' Mum said. 'Kelly, are you staying for tea?'

'What is for tea?'

'Fish and mashed potato.'

Joe groaned. Fish was another of Granpa's favourites.

'Sorry, gotta fly,' said Kelly. She whispered to Joe, 'I can't make it tomorrow. Swimming club. And netball the day after. But I'll leave the games with you!'

Joe grinned. He could put up with fish and mashed potato; he could even put up with Granpa

34

humphing at the tea table. All that mattered to him now was Megamouse. With Megamouse on his side, he need never lose a game again!

7

Joe spent the next three days in a trance. He wandered around school with a dreamy half-smile on his face. His teacher was exasperated: his friends tapped their heads.

'Mad!' they said. 'Joe's flipped!'

Joe didn't care. All through school, he was just waiting to go home, waiting for that magical moment when he sat in Granpa's chair and started up his computer. Waiting for those words to appear on the screen.

'GREETING, LIGHT HAND! WHAT SHALL WE PLAY NOW?'

And then, for the next hour or two, he was in another world. A world where he was a hero, a champion. His score ran into hundreds of thousands. Even Granpa's grumbling couldn't make him feel bad . . .

In fact, Granpa wasn't grumbling so much this week. There was a spring in his step. Miss Tree came to see him every evening, and Joe could hear them talking and laughing together in Granpa's study. Before, he might have felt jealous – but now, he didn't care. He didn't need Granpa. He had Megamouse!

Sometimes, sitting at Granpa's desk after school, he felt as if a pair of hostile eyes were watching him. But when he turned there was nobody there – except, once, Hogarth at the window.

'You spend too much time on that computer,' said Mum to him one evening. 'Switch the computer off and come and help me with Rose! You'll turn into a zombie.'

'But, Mum, it's educational! I'm getting really good at Maths Hound and Spelling Bee!' This was, after all, quite true.

Joe felt a tiny pang of guilt as he switched off the computer. It wasn't guilt about Granpa. He didn't care about Granpa, these days; his head was buzzing with Roadhog Racers ...

No. The guilt was about Megamouse. He'd hardly said HALLO to Megamouse this afternoon, before launching straight into a game.

'Never mind,' Joe told himself. 'I'll talk to him more tomorrow. Anyway, he likes winning games just as much as I do!'

He replaced Megamouse in his box and put him carefully back on the right spot on the shelf. Then he hurried out. The study fell silent.

'Well?' said Cleo. 'Enjoying yourself?' She unlatched her cage and nosed along the desk, looking for crumbs and dead spiders. Joe had left a sweet-wrapper on the desk. Cleo carefully dropped it into the bin. Though I don't know why I bother, she thought. I should just let Granpa tell him off.

'Me score winning top champion super high score!' squeaked Megamouse happily from his shelf. 'Me like *Roadhog Racers*! Win every time.' His Rat grammar still wasn't very good, but Cleo understood him well enough. She shook her head.

'You'll make that boy a games addict,' she said.

'Why?' Megamouse flicked his tail.

'You shouldn't let him win every point.'

'Why not?'

Cleo sat on the mouse mat and glared at him with sharp eyes.

'It's not good for him, that's why not!'

Megamouse pondered. 'Not good?'

'Not good at all!' said Cleo. 'People don't win all the time in real life.'

'Light Hand like win happy,' said Megamouse.

'It's not him winning! It's *you*!'

'Winning easy,' said Megamouse. '*Viking Raiders* easy, *Roadhog Racers* easy. *Martian Warlord* easy easy easy.'

'Really!' sniffed Cleo.

'All too easy. Want big game,' said Megamouse longingly.

'What big game?'

'Outside! Play Outside!' pleaded Megamouse.

'That's no game,' retorted Cleo. 'That's real life!'

'Want big real life,' said Megamouse stubbornly. 'Win Outside for Light Hand.' He scanned the view through the patio door hungrily.

On the far side of the glass, someone trotted into view. A flat nose pressed itself against the glass; two piggy eyes glared at Cleo.

Megamouse recognised that dog now. Its waddle was just the same as on screen. Only the spots were missing.

'Maths Hound!' he squeaked with pleasure. 'Look, Maths Hound play Outside! Me play with Maths Hound.'

'That's not Maths Hound! That's Hogarth.'

'Is,' said Megamouse obstinately. 'Maths Hound!' he squeaked loudly. 'Five times eight? Eleven times three? He not answer.'

'He can't hear you,' said Cleo.

'Sums too easy,' said Megamouse. He tried again. 'Maths Hound! Square root two hundred and eighty five?'

'He's *not* Maths Hound,' said Cleo firmly. 'He's a real dog, in real life! Don't you go anywhere near him! He's dangerous.'

Megamouse felt confused. Why was a Real Dog dangerous? Why didn't Light Hand win in Real Life? What *was* Real Life? It must be the hardest game of all.

Along his circuits ran a flicker of unease. He

hadn't been programmed to play Real Life. He needed to learn more. He wanted to get things right and be a good mouse.

'Winning bad for Light Hand in Real Life?' he wondered aloud. 'Me not good mouse win?'

'You should stop winning all the time,' said Cleo sternly. 'Then you'll be a good mouse.'

'Stop winning all the time,' repeated Megamouse. He ran the problem through his logic circuits. No matter how he analysed it, there was only one solution that he could see.

He would have to start to lose.

8

'Friday, Friday!' sang Joe. 'Oh, it's Friday! Wonderful Friday!'

He dumped his rucksack on the kitchen floor, kicked off his shoes, tickled a giggling Rose on the tummy, and grabbed a packet of crisps from the cupboard on his way out of the kitchen.

'Where are you going, Joe?'

'Just on the computer, Mum!'

'Oh, Joe! Why not go outside instead?'

'But I might not get to play on the computer all weekend, if Granpa's home,' wheedled Joe. 'Just half an hour! Please! Kelly's coming round!'

'Half an hour is all you get,' said Mum. 'Remember Granpa's home early on a Friday.'

'Okay!'

Joe ran into the study, where glory awaited him. But first he would try and talk to Megamouse properly, as he'd promised himself. He offered Cleo a crisp, which she refused.

'Suit yourself,' said Joe. 'Who cares about a grumpy old rat, anyway? Here's my favourite mouse!' Carefully he took Megamouse from his box, plugged him in – and there it was again, the strange sensation of someone watching, and a *noise* – faint, but definitely there.

Joe spun out of his chair, ran to the patio door and flung it open.

'Hogarth!' Sure enough, the bulldog was scratching away in Mum's flowerbed.

'So sorry!'

Joe jumped. Prunella Tree stood by the wall beside him, casually coiling and uncoiling a lead in her hand.

'Such a nuisance,' she said. 'I really don't know how he gets out. Come along, Hogarth!' she called. Hogarth ignored her completely, and she turned back to Joe.

'Boring old dog,' she said with a smile. 'Your computer looks much more interesting. Is your granpa in?'

'Not yet,' said Joe.

'Would you like to play a game with me? I expect I've got some you've never tried. I could bring them over.'

'No, thanks,' said Joe.

'Go on, Joe! I'm sure you could win easily!' She put a foot on the threshold.

'No, thank you,' said Joe. 'I've got Kelly coming over. Any minute now. Mum only planted those flowers last week.'

He stepped backward into the room, and afraid Miss Tree might follow, quickly shut and locked the door. Then, although Miss Tree was already strolling away, he closed the curtains. He had to put the lamp on before he returned to the computer. But now his good mood was spoiled.

'IT'S ME, MEGAMOUSE,' he typed in.

'ME MEGAMOUSE, YOU LIGHT HAND.'

'Yes, yes,' said Joe impatiently.

'ME BAD MOUSE?'

Joe was taken aback. 'WHAT DO YOU MEAN?'

'MEGAMOUSE BAD. NOT GOOD WINNING ALL GAMES.'

Joe frowned. What was Megamouse getting at? Why did he think he was bad at winning games? He was very good at it.

'MEGAMOUSE BAD FOR WINNING GAMES FOR LIGHT HAND, BAD FOR LIGHT HAND WINNING GAMES IN REAL LIFE!'

'WHAT?'

'WIN WIN WIN GAMES ALL TIME BAD FOR LIGHT HAND. BAD MEGAMOUSE MAKE LIGHT HAND WIN WIN WIN.'

'STOP! I DON'T UNDERSTAND,' typed Joe. He was getting exasperated. What on earth was Megamouse going on about?

'LIGHT HAND LIKE PLAY OUTSIDE?'

'YES,' replied Joe, relieved that at last there was something he could understand. 'LATER. PLAY *ROADHOG RACERS* NOW.' He decided to put off talking to Megamouse for the moment. He wasn't in the mood to try and make sense of all this. He wanted to play games and win, to be a computer superstar – not an ordinary boy who was all thumbs on a keyboard and couldn't spell *cabbage*.

'*ROADHOG RACERS*!' he repeated, because Megamouse was slow to respond.

The Racers appeared on the screen. Joe breathed a deep sigh of pleasure, picked his favourite red car, and sat back to enjoy the game.

But this time, things didn't turn out as he expected. His car was slow off the mark. It bounced off a wall of tyres, spun, clipped a green car, rolled over and crashed.

Joe was stunned. What had gone wrong? He hadn't even reached the second corner, and he was out of the game!

'NEW RACE!' he ordered. This time, he picked a blue car, but it fared no better than the first. Joe couldn't control it. It veered straight off the track and hit a wall.

There was a strange noise from Cleo's cage: a tiny snort, as if the white rat was laughing.

'Shut up, Cleo!' said Joe. 'START *VIKING RAIDERS*!'

It was a slaughter. He didn't have a chance to collect a single magic ring, or even to wield his sword, Trollbiter, before his head was chopped off by a battle-axe.

'This is terrible!' wailed Joe. His fingers punched at the keyboard.

'MEGAMOUSE – WHAT'S WRONG?'

'NOTHING WRONG. ALL RIGHT.'

'NO! PLAY *MARTIAN WARLORD*!'

'Joe?'

Kelly ventured into the study, to find Joe being drowned in gollops of poisonous slime.

'You're losing, Joe! How come?'

'I don't know!' said Joe furiously. 'I'm losing *everything*!' He thumped the keyboard in frustration.

'Let me try.' Kelly restarted *Martian Warlord*. She zapped the aliens with no trouble.

'Don't see a problem there,' she said, giving Megamouse back to Joe. The instant Joe laid his hand on the mouse's back, a Martian laser blasted him to bits.

'You see? It's hopeless!' Angrily he typed in,

'MEGAMOUSE! WHY AM I LOSING?'

'LOSING GOOD WINNING BAD FOR LIGHT HAND. GOOD LOSE GOOD MOUSE.'

'NO!' Joe banged on the desk so hard that Cleo's cage rattled.

'Hey, Joe – ' began Kelly.

'BAD MOUSE! BAD MOUSE!' typed Joe furiously, stabbing the keyboard. 'Stupid mouse!' he cried.

'Joe! Stop!' wailed Kelly.

Joe spun round. In his anger, he hadn't heard the door open. He hadn't noticed Granpa standing there.

'Sounds like a lot of noise for Spelling Bee,' said Granpa. He put down his briefcase. 'Actually, that doesn't look like Spelling Bee to me.' He looked at Joe questioningly.

'It's, um, *Martian Warlord*,' stammered Kelly. 'I lent it to Joe.'

'Oh, yes?' The bristly eyebrows shot upwards. 'Did I say you could play *Martian Warlord* on my computer?' He caught sight of the mouse under Joe's hand, and stiffened. His voice turned cold. 'And did I say you could use the Megamouse?'

'No,' Joe muttered.

'We just borrowed it for a bit,' said Kelly. 'We were being very careful.'

'Were you? It didn't look to me as if Joe was being very careful.'

'It wins games for us,' explained Kelly.

'Does it, indeed? Then let's see it win!'

'It's not doing it today,' said Joe.

'Hrmph!' snorted Granpa, as he started up Spelling Bee. 'Your mother tells me you've been in here every day this week. You should be an expert at Spelling Bee by now – Megamouse or no Megamouse.'

'*Surprise!*' buzzed Spelling Bee. As soon as Joe touched the keyboard, the answer spelled itself out.

46

'SIRPRFYZS!&#.'

'Very funny,' said Granpa frostily. 'Let's try Maths Hound, shall we? See what Megamouse can do for you there.'

Maths Hound waddled on-screen.

'48 x 6 = ?' he asked.

'2¾,' came the reply.

Granpa glowered. 'I can see it was a complete waste of my time showing you those computer games!'

'But I didn't give that answer!' said Joe desperately. 'It was Megamouse!'

'I've had enough of this,' said Granpa. He snapped the off switch. 'Do you take me for a complete fool?'

'But Granpa, it's true!'

'You are banned from this computer, Joe. And so are your friends.' He glared at Kelly, who shuffled towards the door and sidled out. Granpa turned back to Joe. 'This equipment's too valuable for you to fool around on! I am very disappointed!'

'But Granpa, I wasn't fooling around – '

'You knew you weren't supposed to touch the Megamouse!'

Joe's throat felt tight. He *had* known. The anger in Granpa's voice made him shrivel up inside.

'But Granpa, you don't understand – '

'If I have any more trouble over this computer, Joe, I may have to make myself very unpleasant!'

47

'You already are,' said Joe.

Granpa's head jerked back. 'What's that?'

'I said, you already are!' The words began to flood out of Joe, tumbling over themselves in their hurry to be said. He didn't try to stop them. He'd been thinking them for too long.

'You boss Dad around something rotten and you treat Mum like a servant even though they're always nice as pie to you and you're always going on about how stupid we all are and how clever you are and how important your work is when Dad's the best dad and you're the meanest grandad making us eat mashed potato all the time and hogging the big TV and expecting Rose to stop crying just for you when you never even smile at her and – and being rude and horrible to everybody!'

Joe ran out of breath. He waited for the explosion, but Granpa didn't answer. He just stood and stared at Joe, his expression quite unreadable.

Joe heard his own words echoing round and round the room. He couldn't believe he'd said them – but he couldn't unsay them now.

'Sorry, Granpa,' he muttered. Then he turned and fled.

9

Megamouse sat tight on his mouse mat. He dared not move, nor squeak, nor even twitch his tail. Cleo squeaked softly at him, but received no answer. When Granpa's big hand picked him up to inspect him, Megamouse kept quite still. When Granpa typed into the computer, Megamouse was dumb. The screen stayed blank.

'Hrmph!' Granpa rumbled at last. He replaced Megamouse on his mat, and with stiff fingers unlocked Cleo's cage.

'Not horrible to you, am I, old girl?'

Cleo nibbled his fingers politely, and tried to nudge him towards the digestive biscuits. But Granpa just stared into space.

Mum put her head round the door.

'Is everything all right? I thought I heard voices . . . '

'Yes,' said Granpa.

'Joe's not been messing around in here, has he?'

'No.'

'That's good. I was a bit worried . . . He does so enjoy using your computer. He's been over the moon with it the last few days. As long as he's not

49

causing you any trouble . . . Is steak all right for your tea?'

'Yes,' said Granpa. After a moment he added, 'Thank you.' But Mum had already left the room.

Granpa drummed his fingers on the table.

'Hrmph!' he said eventually. Then he stood up awkwardly, gathered his crutches and stomped out.

'Well!' said Cleo to Megamouse. 'I think you overdid that a bit. Not quite what I meant.'

'You say me not win all games,' squeaked Megamouse.

'Yes, but I didn't mean – oh, well. It's too late now.'

'Light Hand say me bad mouse,' said Megamouse dolefully.

'He's just a bit upset.'

'Me bad mouse!'

'No, no,' said Cleo. 'I'm sure he'll come round.'

'Bad, bad,' wailed Megamouse. 'Me no good real mouse, bad computer mouse, no good ever.'

'Maybe you should have let him win one game.'

'Me lose everything.' Megamouse gazed sadly across the room to the patio doors. The curtains were still pulled across them.

'Light Hand like play Outside,' he remembered. 'Me play Outside for Light Hand! Me win Outside for Light Hand! Me learn Real Life! Then Light Hand say good mouse, good mouse.'

'Now hang on! You don't understand –'

Cleo found she was talking to nobody. Megamouse had plunged off the desk and landed on the carpet with a faint thud.

'Outside!' he squeaked, as he dived under the bed.

Cursing, Cleo hastily unlatched her cage and scrambled down to the floor after him. He was already rolling through the dust to the hole in the skirting-board. Before she could catch up, he had scuttled through it and was out of sight.

Cleo scampered across the floor and pushed through the hole after him.

'I'm too old for this sort of thing!' she grumbled, as flakes of plaster fell on to her back.

Ahead of her, Megamouse squeezed through a gap, past a broken air-brick, and found himself outside.

A cool breeze blew. A hundred strange sounds vibrated through his circuits. And his optic cells went into overload.

Outside was *enormous*. It was a million times bigger than any game he'd ever seen.

'Big big *big*!' Hurriedly Megamouse clicked his button to make it smaller. Everything stayed exactly the same size.

A bright yellow circle overhead was hurting his optic cells.

'Delete,' said Megamouse firmly, and wondered why the sun refused to be deleted.

A huge mouse mat was spread before him; a vast carpet of green. Venturing on to it, Megamouse discovered that it was uncomfortably prickly. He looked around, bemused. Tiny creatures scuttled around him on many legs, busy playing this big game of Outside that Megamouse didn't understand. Other creatures whirred and buzzed past his head.

'Who you?' he asked. 'Spelling Bee? F-L-I-G-H-T, flight.' But Spelling Bee ignored him and buzzed away.

'Megamouse!' hissed Cleo from the shadow of the wall. She glanced around warily. 'Come back!'

Megamouse tried to roll away, but grass kept catching under his little wheel. With an effort he made it to the edge of the lawn.

'Not like green mouse mat. Hard surface good,' he decided as he trundled across the path.

'And
    flat
       surface
         better,'

he added as he juddered down the steps to the drive,

'But   surface   of
    smooth   best   all,'

he finished, jolting painfully over the pitted tarmac. Every dent was like a ditch to him, and every bump a hill. But he had to learn to play Outside for Light

Hand. And when he got to the end of the drive, it was worth the journey.

Megamouse sat at the gate, transfixed with wonder. Enormous shapes of dazzling red and green and gold sped past, making the ground shake. The air throbbed with the roar of engines.

He knew this game! It even had the roadworks with their yellow barriers – just like on his screen.

'*Roadhog Racers*!' squealed Megamouse delightedly. 'Big big Racers! Me *good* at *Roadhog Racers*! Me win 9000 points!'

He rolled out into the road, clicking his button excitedly.

'Come back!' cried Cleo from the kerb. Her voice was drowned out by the roar of the Racers.

'Turn round! Go left!' Megamouse commanded the Racers. To his surprise, they did not swerve. 'Slow down! *Stop*!'

The Racers did not stop. They hurtled straight past him with a rush of air that nearly bowled him over. Megamouse clicked his buttons busily – in vain. The Racers would not obey.

'Error! Error!' he cried. 'Abandon game!'

Beneath him the ground vibrated. A huge green Racer was rushing towards him, growing bigger and bigger . . .

'Help!' squeaked Megamouse. 'Too big! Escape! Delete!' But no matter how frantically he clicked, the monster kept on coming.

There was a deafening noise, and a whirlwind of hot air as the lorry hurtled past. Megamouse was sent spinning helplessly round in a circle.

'My circuits are jamming!' he thought dizzily.

Two more cars were thundering towards him from opposite directions. Megamouse couldn't control these mighty Racers. And if he was caught beneath a wheel he would end up in as many crumbs as a digestive biscuit.

'No no no delete delete delete!' he wailed. 'Not like this game! Close down! *Close down*!' Desperately he tried to dart out of the Racers' way. 'Want Cleo!' he whimpered. 'Want Light Hand! Want nice quiet sums!'

Then something grabbed him by the tail, and dragged him backwards off the road, away from the roaring, crushing Racers. He found himself being jolted over the kerb and dumped on the pavement. Weak and shaken, he turned to see who had rescued him.

'Cleo?' he whispered thankfully.

A large, wet nose prodded at his shell. His rescuer wasn't Cleo. It was Hogarth.

10

'He isn't staying for much longer, is he?' asked Kelly.

'Months.' Joe's voice was muffled. He leaned on his bedroom window-sill, his face buried in his arms.

'*Months*?'

Joe raised his head to gaze out of the window. 'Months,' he said dully.

'Well, maybe you could just stay out of his way?' suggested Kelly.

'How can I? He's taken over the house!'

'You can always come over to my place,' said Kelly. 'Cheer up, Joe.' She gave him an awkward pat on the shoulder, then turned to look out of the window with him. Together they stared down at the roadworks, where a workman was just pouring himself a mug of tea from a thermos.

'I wish Dad would come home,' said Joe softly.

'Look,' said Kelly, trying to distract him. 'There's Miss Tree. Isn't that a stupid name? If she was called Holly, she'd be Holly Tree.'

'She isn't stupid,' said Joe. 'She's clever. Much cleverer than me. Granpa likes her.'

'Or if her name was Cherry,' Kelly persevered,

'she'd be Cherry Tree. I wonder where she's going. Maybe she's after Horrible Hogarth. Look, there he is! What's he doing?' Kelly pressed her face to the window. Then she cried out in alarm.

'Oh, no! He's run right into the road! Stop, Hogarth! He's going to get run over! Why is she just standing there?' yelled Kelly.

She flew out of the room, and thudded down the stairs. Joe peered out of the window.

Kelly was right – Miss Tree was just standing there, while cars beeped and honked and swerved to avoid Hogarth. Soon there was a traffic jam – and there was Dad's white van in the middle of it, with the ladders tied on top.

Drivers wound down their windows and shouted angrily, while Miss Tree, on the pavement, began to laugh. Hogarth dodged the cars and galloped across the road. Something dangled from his mouth, by a string . . . or perhaps a wire . . .

Joe's heart turned over.

'Megamouse!' He dashed from the window and leapt down the stairs three at a time.

'Hogarth!' called Miss Tree. 'Here, boy!' As the bulldog waddled past the roadworks, he yelped suddenly and let Megamouse fall. Cleo's sharp teeth had just attacked his broad behind. Hogarth twisted round, barking. He forgot Megamouse and pounced on Cleo, pinning her to the ground with a heavy paw.

56

'Hogarth!' yelled Kelly.

'Megamouse!' cried Joe, as they both ran for the roadworks.

'Oy, there!' shouted the startled workman, dropping his cup of tea.

But Miss Tree got there first.

'Stupid dog!' she said. 'Not the rat – the *mouse*! Get the mouse!' She lunged at Megamouse. He slipped through her fingers – but he couldn't roll far. He was trapped, with Miss Tree on one side, and a hole in the road on the other.

There was only one way he could go.

Megamouse hesitated for a second – then he rolled to the brink of the hole, and toppled in. Joe and Kelly came pounding up, too late. Megamouse was gone.

As Miss Tree stared at the hole, angry and baffled, a white rat shot between her legs. With a despairing squeal, Cleo plunged after Megamouse. They disappeared into the darkness.

Four stunned faces stared at the hole in the road. The workman was the first to recover.

'This isn't a playground!' he said. 'Back behind the barriers, all of you!'

Dad came hurrying up.

'Joe? What's going on? I saw a rat, or something . . .'

Joe pointed a shaky hand at the hole.

'Dad – it's Megamouse! He's in there – and Cleo – we've got to get them out!'

Miss Tree's boot tapped impatiently. 'What's down there?' she snapped at the workman.

'Eh? Sewers.'

'Where's the next exit?'

'There are manholes all over the place – there's one up the road, one by the traffic lights – '

'Right!' said Miss Tree. 'Hogarth? Down you go!'

And taking the unhappy bulldog by the scruff of the neck, she hurled him down the hole. There was an echoing howl and a thud. Miss Tree threw back her head and laughed.

'Oh!' cried Kelly. 'How could you? You pig!'

Miss Tree shrugged. 'All in the game,' she said, stalking away.

Kelly leaned over the edge, but Dad pulled her back. 'Oh, no you don't!'

'*I'll* fish him out,' offered the workman. Carefully he descended into the hole. A moment later he reappeared, shaking his head.

'He's gone. I think he's in the tunnel heading that way.' He pointed towards the traffic lights. 'I can't see him, but I can hear him barking. It's a maze down there, though – you'll be lucky to get him out.'

'Can't *you* reach him?' begged Kelly.

'Sorry, lass! I can't squeeze through those tunnels.'

'But we've got to save him!'

'And Megamouse!' cried Joe. 'We've got to rescue Megamouse!' He felt sick with misery and fear. He began to run towards the distant traffic lights. He didn't even know if he was going the right way – but he had to do *something*.

A hundred metres on, he was overtaken by a silver jeep. The driver was Miss Tree, her hair blowing behind her like a black flag. She sped past, waving gaily to him.

'Finders keepers! Losers weepers!' she shouted.

'I hate her!' panted Kelly, pounding up behind Joe. 'She shouldn't be allowed to keep a dog! Hang on, Joe. I've got a stitch.' She halted and touched her toes. Then she gasped.

'I can hear Hogarth!' Kneeling by a storm drain, she put her ear close to the grid. 'It *is* Hogarth! He sounds excited – as if he's chasing something!'

'Megamouse,' whispered Joe, a painful hope piercing his heart.

He squatted down to listen. From underground there came the faintest echo of distant barking, as if from a phantom dog, buried deep in the earth.

11

Loud and close behind Cleo the barks rang out. Their echoes boomed relentlessly down the tunnel walls, until Megamouse felt as if he were trapped inside a cage of noise.

'Don't worry – he won't keep it up for long,' puffed Cleo. 'Hear him floundering about? Just keep going!'

Megamouse rolled along the jutting, slimy ledge that travelled the length of the sewer tunnel. One slip and he'd be sinking in the foul stream that flowed sluggishly alongside . . .

'It doesn't half smell down here,' gasped Cleo. 'And they say *rats* live in the sewers! How they put up with this stink beats me!'

Behind them, the thunderous barking turned to a terrified howl, and a splash.

'Told you so,' said Cleo smugly. 'Come on, Megamouse! Don't stop now! What's the matter?'

Megamouse was slowing. His wheel was clogged with slime – but that wasn't the only reason why he felt so drowsy and weak.

His batteries were running down. He had never

rolled so far before; and there was nowhere for him to recharge.

'Need food,' he murmured.

'Food?' said Cleo. 'Oh, heck! Just keep going, Megamouse. Keep going for as long as you can! We'll find a way up soon!'

Megamouse tried, but he felt his energy draining away with every metre. His optic cells were failing: darkness was closing in on him. His wheel squeaked pitifully.

'Want Light Hand,' he whimpered mournfully. 'Want nice soft mouse mat.'

'Don't stop! Don't stop!' entreated Cleo. 'Or the dog will catch us up!'

But Megamouse stopped dead.

Half-conscious as he was, he felt something calling to him. A high, entrancing song hummed through a crack in the crumbling brickwork of the tunnel.

'Food!' sighed Megamouse. Gathering his last shreds of strength, he pushed into the crack. There, like a huge snake, hissing and buzzing, lay a thick electric cable. As Megamouse came close, a spark jumped from it.

Something had already gnawed part way through the cable, so that the wires were exposed, humming with electricity. Megamouse rested his tail on the singing wires and drank from the current. Electricity coursed through his circuits like fire.

'Wow,' said Cleo, backing away – for this was

high-voltage stuff. A hundred sparks sprang from the cable and lit up the darkness.

All around her, illuminated by the sizzling fountains of sparks, Cleo saw a sight that made her heart stand still.

Rats!

Massive, muscled, menacing sewer rats. She hadn't known rats could be so *big* – each one was twice her size. Their fur bristled; their red eyes glittered.

'Er – well, hallo there, cousins – ' began Cleo, and got no further.

The biggest rat pounced.

It leapt on Megamouse's back, and its teeth crunched on his casing. Megamouse felt the plastic crack. The rat was too heavy for him to shake off.

But he was still wired up to the electric cable. As the sewer rat's long teeth grazed his circuits, there was a crackling blue flash. The sewer rat was thrown across the tunnel. It lay still, stunned by several hundred volts.

'Get out of our way,' hissed Cleo to the other rats, 'or the same thing will happen to *you*!'

Slowly the brown horde parted to let Cleo and Megamouse through; but Cleo heard them rustling as they closed up again behind her, ready to attack.

Then she heard something else. A splashing and crashing; a growling and grumbling; the bad-tempered wheezing of a wet but stubborn bulldog.

The rats heard him too, and turned to flee – but Hogarth had their scent. It was a scent that even he couldn't miss. He charged.

As Cleo and Megamouse fled down the tunnel, a flurry of squeals and snarls echoed behind them.

'Now's our chance!' said Cleo. 'Hurry!'

Megamouse couldn't hurry. Most of the electric charge he'd drunk from the cable had gone straight through him into the sewer rat – his batteries were almost as flat as before. Just fifty metres further on, he ground gently to a halt.

'No move,' he whispered.

Cleo sniffed. She could smell fresh air! Looking up, she saw a trickle of daylight leaking through a cracked manhole. There might be just enough space for a rat to squeeze through. But it was a long climb up.

'I can't,' sighed Cleo. She felt as tired as she'd ever been in her life. She gathered all her strength together, then, grasping Megamouse by the tail, clambered slowly up the ragged walls, clinging to jutting stones and lumps of tarmac. Once or twice she nearly fell; but at last, with a huge effort, she reached the top, and hauled Megamouse up after her. They were out of the sewer.

Cleo lay in the gutter, feeling the cool breeze rush over her with immense relief. Half-blinded by the sunlight, she wearily lifted her head and saw above her Prunella Tree's eager, hungry smile.

12

'Look at that!' exclaimed Kelly. 'The traffic lights are going crazy!'

Ahead of them, the lights flashed red and green in rapid succession, as Megamouse struggled with the sewer rat below.

Then the lights went out altogether. Brakes screeched. All the traffic stopped dead – except a silver jeep that swerved up onto the pavement and skidded past the other cars.

The jeep juddered to a sudden halt, and Joe saw Miss Tree spring out and stoop to the ground. Picking something up, she held it aloft triumphantly; a small, grey shape, dangling from a long tail.

'Megamouse!' yelled Joe. Miss Tree looked up and smiled.

'You lose,' she said. Joe saw Cleo creep away, ignored by Miss Tree; for just then, there was a hollow bark. Miss Tree kicked aside the broken manhole cover, and a filthy, sodden, very tired bulldog slowly hauled himself out onto the road. He stood before her, dripping slime and wagging his stumpy tail, and proudly dropped a large dead rat at her feet.

'Hogarth! You disgusting dog!' Miss Tree kicked the rat away. 'No – you are certainly *not* coming with me!' She flung herself into the jeep. The door slammed, shutting Hogarth out, and the jeep pulled away.

'Stop!' cried Joe. 'Bring back Megamouse!' Despite his aching legs, he chased after it as it accelerated away. He couldn't keep up, though. As the jeep drove out of sight he halted, gasping for breath.

'Joe! Come back!' called Dad. Joe walked heavily back to where he stood with Kelly and Hogarth. There was no sign of Cleo. Joe found his sight blurring with tears of frustration and grief.

'Don't worry,' said Dad, putting his arm around Joe. 'I've got her registration number. The police will track her down.'

'We've got to rescue Megamouse!' cried Joe. He felt responsible for Megamouse. *He* was the one who had brought him to life – the only one who had believed in him . . .'

'What am I going to say to Granpa?' he said despairingly.

'Leave that to me,' said Dad. 'The Megamouse *does* move by itself, Joe, doesn't it? Almost as if it's got a life of its own.'

Joe couldn't answer. He leaned against Dad's shoulder.

'We'll get it back,' Dad assured him.

'Yes,' said Joe sadly. He knew he would never see Megamouse again.

Kelly was on her knees, hugging a shivering Hogarth.

'*Brave* dog!' she told him. 'Fancy her calling you disgusting! *She's* the disgusting one.'

'You're filthy,' said Joe dully. Kelly's clothes were smeared with slime.

'So?' said Kelly defiantly. 'I'm going to take Hogarth home and give him a good wash. You'd like a nice bath, wouldn't you, Hogarth?'

Hogarth looked despondent.

'And a rub down with a warm towel by the fire?'

Hogarth perked up a little.

'And a bowl of nice meaty chunks for your supper?'

Hogarth's stumpy tail began to wag.

'That's a good dog!'

'We'd better take him back with us, then,' said Joe wearily. His heart ached. What would become of Megamouse? Where was he? Was he frightened? Was he hurt? If only Joe hadn't been so intent on winning everything, he might not have lost Megamouse.

I was Megamouse's only friend, thought Joe. And I've let him down.

13

At first, Granpa didn't believe Dad's story. But there was no doubt that Megamouse had gone, and so had Miss Tree; and that Dad had seen the one carry off the other.

'She was so friendly,' said Granpa gruffly. 'Thought she liked me.'

'So did I,' agreed Dad. 'What I don't understand is what she wants with the Megamouse. Is it valuable?'

Granpa nodded reluctantly. 'If it really can move, then it's worth a lot of money... I should have tested it. I should have known. Now she'll sell it. She's an industrial spy – steals other people's work.'

'Then we'll never get Megamouse back!' cried Joe.

'Don't give up yet!' Dad told him. 'I'll ring the police now and see if they can help.' He hurried out, leaving Granpa and Joe alone together.

'I shouldn't have trusted Miss Tree,' said Granpa fiercely. 'Should have known she wouldn't really want to be friends with an old codger like me. How could I have been so stupid?'

'You weren't stupid,' said Joe, trying to cheer him up. 'You weren't to know.'

Granpa shook his head. 'I should have known. That mouse is a prototype – the only one of its kind. At least nothing else is missing . . .'

His eye fell upon Cleo's empty cage.

'Cleo?' Granpa anxiously riffled through her nest of sawdust, and then looked frantically around the room. 'Where's Cleo?'

'She followed Megamouse down the hole in the road,' Joe told him. He'd been so busy worrying about Megamouse that he'd forgotten about Cleo. 'She came out again,' he added, seeing the horror on Granpa's face. 'I saw her by the road, near Miss Tree. But when Miss Tree drove off, Cleo wasn't there. I don't know where she went – she must have run away.'

'Cleo,' breathed Granpa. He sat down on his bed, looking suddenly much older. His hands were trembling.

Joe was astonished to see Granpa looking so shaken. Cleo was only a rat, after all, and not a very nice one at that. A rat could look after itself, better than Megamouse could . . .

Then it dawned on him that Granpa felt just the same way about Cleo as Joe did about Megamouse. *Terrible.*

Cautiously he reached for Granpa's hand. It felt thin and cold.

'She's a clever rat, Granpa,' Joe said reassuringly. 'She'll be all right.' He patted Granpa's hand awkwardly, not knowing what else to say to cheer him up. He rummaged in his pocket. 'Do you want a toffee?'

'Thanks,' said Granpa gruffly. He detached one from the sticky mass in the bag and chewed in downcast silence. After a while he said, 'Miss Tree didn't really like me at all, did she? Just wanted to find out what I knew.'

'I expect she liked you as well,' said Joe.

Granpa shook his head, sighing. 'What I need is a cup of tea.'

'I'll go and ask Mum,' offered Joe.

'I can make myself a cup of tea,' said Granpa haughtily. 'Don't want to treat your mother like a servant, do we?'

Joe bit his lip. 'I didn't really mean all that!'

'Yes, you did,' said Granpa, 'and I don't blame you. Thing is, I'm better with numbers than people. Always have been. More comfortable with a computer. You know where you are with a computer.' He stood up. 'Come on. You show me where you keep the tea.'

They found Mum in the kitchen, feeding Rose. Granpa made a pot of tea, with Joe's help, and poured a cup for her. Mum looked surprised, but pleased. She sat Rose on Granpa's knee while she found the biscuits, and Joe tickled Rose's toes to make sure she didn't cry. Granpa looked rather alarmed to be holding Rose. His eyebrows bristled like anything.

Dad came in carrying the phone book, a serious expression on his face.

'Bad news,' he said. 'The police say Miss Tree's car must have a false registration. They can't trace her. And there are no Trees at all in the phone book! Not one.'

'There should be at least two,' protested Joe. 'Her house next door, and her cottage at Acrefield!'

Dad shook his head. 'She must use a false name as well.'

'How do you know she's got a cottage?' asked Mum.

'She told us. Dad!' cried Joe. 'She might have gone there! Can we go and look?'

'Acrefield's a big place,' said Dad. 'We could try – but we might drive around all day and not find her! Unless we know exactly where to go, we haven't much chance of tracking her down.'

The back door burst open, and Kelly bounced in, dragging a reluctant Hogarth.

'Isn't he beautiful? Doesn't he gleam?' she said proudly.

Hogarth was sleek and spotless. He smelt strongly of peach shampoo. He made straight for the kitchen bin, and tried to stick his head in it.

'Come out, silly Hogarth!' said Kelly indulgently.

'I think he's a really clever dog. Did you see how he spotted the bin straight away?'

'Incredible,' said Mum.

'It took ages to get all the dirt off him, but he only tried to bite me twice,' said Kelly admiringly. 'I wish he was mine!'

'It's a shame he belongs to Miss Tree . . .' Joe paused, staring at Hogarth as an idea dawned.

'Maybe we *have* got a chance of tracking her down,' he said thoughtfully. 'Maybe Hogarth knows where she is! Good dog! Clever Hogarth!'

14

Cleo had a rough ride.

She'd managed to jump into the jeep without Miss Tree seeing. Now, crouched in the back, her claws digging into the mat, she was thrown from side to side every time the jeep went round a corner.

By the time it stopped, Cleo felt quite sick. She had just enough presence of mind to slip out behind Miss Tree, before the door slammed shut. Cowering under a wheel, she watched Miss Tree walking up to a small, overgrown cottage, half-hidden amongst tall trees.

Darkness was falling. Strange smells assailed Cleo's nose: damp earth, manure and wood-smoke . . . Country smells.

'What am I doing here?' she thought. 'Miles from anywhere! I'm a lab rat! I don't know anything about the country. I must be mad!' The cottage door closed behind Miss Tree. 'And I'm shut out!'

As Cleo crept wearily up the path, she felt old, battered and very hungry. A brown mouse popped up from behind a broken flowerpot to watch her with beady black eyes.

'You'm new round hereabouts,' it declared.

'That's right,' said Cleo cautiously, wary of strangers after her encounter with the sewer rats.

But the mouse just sucked on a straw. 'You'm a tadge clarty,' it remarked.

'Well, well,' said Cleo, not having the slightest idea what it was talking about.

'*Mud*,' said the mouse.

'Oh! Yes. Is there a way in?'

'Ah,' said the mouse. It chewed its straw. 'You'm wanting to get in after yon setter of mousetraps?' Cleo could scarcely understand its thick accent. It probably couldn't understand her either, she thought gloomily. Looked a bit dim.

'My friend Megamouse is a prisoner in there,' she said.

To her surprise, the mouse was suddenly alert.

'Mouse? Mouse, you say, prisoner?' It stared at her, then seemed to come to a decision. 'I be Bartle. You come along with me. This way, quick!'

Bartle disappeared behind a thorny bush and up a drainpipe. Cleo followed. She found herself underneath the sink in a cold, stone-flagged kitchen. Mousetraps were scattered at random across the floor.

'She be upstairs,' said Bartle quietly. 'This way, through the fireplace. She don't never have no fire.'

He scampered across the stone flags to the old-fashioned hearth. Cleo pattered after him, keeping her tail away from the mousetraps. She didn't like the look of this place. But she had to find Megamouse.

Bartle disappeared into the fireplace, and scrambled nimbly up the broken brickwork of the chimney. Cleo's heart sank.

'Not more climbing!' she thought. 'I've had enough of that for one day!' Heaving a sigh, she laboured up the chimney, emerging in a smaller fireplace upstairs.

And then she saw him.

The floorboards were bare. A camp bed and a canvas chair were the only furniture. A suitcase lay on the dusty floor, with a computer resting on top of it; and next to the computer – but not plugged in – was a still and lifeless Megamouse.

Miss Tree flopped in the creaking chair, her shoes kicked off. She was eating asparagus from a tin and swigging champagne from a bottle. She looked cheerful, but as Bartle darted across the fireplace she swung round and fixed him with a fierce, glittering eye.

'Dratted mice!' She hurled the bottle at him, and it smashed on the hearth. Puddles of champagne lay fizzing among the shards of glass.

Cleo and Bartle quietly retreated to the kitchen.

'What can we do?' said Cleo despairingly. 'We can't reach him while *she's* there!'

'Don't you worry!' Bartle's black eyes glinted.

'Us don't care for yon mouse-catcher. Us'd be glad to see the back of her.'

'Us? Who's *us*?'

'Us mice and rats. Thinks we're stupid, she do. She be wrong.'

'But how can you help?'

'We'll talk together, and think on. If you'm hungry, there be a few kidney beans under the stove . . . not much, but she don't eat proper food. Only horrible stuff in tins. I'll go and find t'others. Never fear, us'll get him out!'

15

Cleo shivered as she crouched in the kitchen fireplace. Bartle was right: it hadn't seen a fire in years. In the room above, Megamouse lay on the suitcase in the dark, while Miss Tree snored on the camp bed.

Before nightfall, Cleo had met a succession of sleek brown rats and neat grey mice, who'd scampered across the kitchen floor to talk to her, then run off to chatter amongst themselves. She felt sure they were cooking up a plan, but no one told her what it was.

Since then, it had been a long, cold night. Cleo had had little sleep. She longed for the rustling warmth of her cage, instead of this chilly hearth . . . and for a big, wrinkled hand to carefully stroke her back, and offer her a digestive biscuit . . .

'Wake up!' said Bartle's voice. ''Tis nearly light.'

Cleo opened bleary eyes, and peered into the surrounding shadows. They were now just dark grey, rather than pitch black.

'Them rats be at work already,' whispered Bartle. 'She be in for a surprise.'

'What sort of surprise?'

'Something to keep her busy!' Bartle chuckled. 'How about a little flood? Them old lead pipes be easy for rats to chew through. So be them wires, them buzzing wires – '

'Electrics? Don't touch them! They're dangerous!' Cleo, now wide awake, shuddered as she recalled the crackle of underground lightning in the sewers.

'Don't 'ee worry! While she's thus distracted, see, we'll rescue yon mouse.'

'He needs to wake up first,' said Cleo. 'Maybe I can plug him in without waking Miss Tree . . . '

'Plug him in?' Bartle was bemused.

'I'll show you.' Cleo scrambled up the narrow chimney, and peered cautiously into the room above.

Miss Tree lay on the camp bed, fully dressed, snoring softly beside an empty champagne bottle. Like a grey wraith in the twilight, Cleo glided to the suitcase. Gently she nudged Megamouse, but there was no response.

'Dead?' whispered Bartle.

'Just sleeping . . . Poor thing. What a state he's in!' Cracked, tooth-pocked and spattered with mud, Megamouse was a woeful sight.

'Strange sort of mouse,' said Bartle, sniffing him doubtfully.

'Oh, yes. Very rare and unusual. In fact,' said Cleo, pulling Megamouse's tail towards the com-

77

puter socket, 'he's probably the only one of his kind in the world.'

She plugged him in and Bartle's eyes widened.

'That be for sure!' he said.

Cleo switched on the hard drive, and Megamouse twitched. His tail quivered. His button clicked once, twice. He swivelled on the suitcase.

'Cleo?' he squeaked. 'Where am I?'

'Miss Tree's cottage. Keep still, Megamouse, and keep quiet! You need to recharge your batteries before we can get you out of here.'

'Okay.' He sat silent, while Miss Tree mumbled in her sleep, tossing on the bed. Bartle glided away, and left Cleo crouching next to Megamouse, and worrying.

Would he have time to recharge before Miss Tree awoke? Then how were they going to get him down that chimney? Megamouse wasn't equipped for climbing.

'Maybe Bartle has a plan,' she thought. But once out of the cottage, they still had to get home... Cleo's heart sank. Where *was* home? How were they to find it?

'Cleo,' whispered Megamouse, 'lots files on this computer.'

'Good. Shush.'

'Lots files, lots numbers... no games. Maybe Light Hand like files? I copy files for Light Hand.'

'All right! Fine! Now shush!'

Megamouse sat quietly once more, now and again clicking faintly. Meanwhile Cleo's sharp ears picked up another, more distant sound: the faraway trickle of water on stone. Light began to shine through the curtainless window, filling the room with a pale, lemon glow.

At any other time Cleo would have been glad to see the dawn. Now she huddled in the computer's shadow, sick with apprehension lest Miss Tree should wake too soon . . .

Miss Tree yawned, stretched and sat up. Cleo froze. But Miss Tree didn't see her. She rubbed her eyes, and groaned:

'Coffee!'

Rolling off the camp bed, she staggered to the door. Cleo heard her stumbling downstairs.

'Come on!' she hissed to Megamouse. 'Are you ready? Time to go!' Bartle reappeared in the fire-place, beckoning them.

'Rats have done their work,' he chuckled. 'There be a lake down there!'

From downstairs came a yell, and a furious splash. Bartle added,

'Rats be working on them wires too – '

The low purr of the computer ceased abruptly.

'Food all gone,' said Megamouse, withdrawing his tail.

'Come on, then! Let's get out of here!' Cleo

darted towards the fireplace, and Megamouse rolled after her.

Miss Tree blundered back in, swearing loudly. Her feet left soggy footprints on the floorboards.

'Dratted place!' she said. 'Dratted pipes!' Then she saw Megamouse, rattling vainly against the edge of the hearth. Although it was less than a centimetre high, that was too much for his little wheel.

Miss Tree threw herself upon him. Megamouse squealed in alarm and shot away across the floor, with Miss Tree pounding after him. He scuttled frantically around the room, zigzagging this way and that, and finally he zoomed under the camp bed.

Miss Tree lifted the bed, tipped it over and snatched him up.

'Got you!' she crowed. Cleo sprang to the floor; at least she could bite Miss Tree in the ankle, if nothing else.

But Miss Tree paused, clutching Megamouse, and sniffed the air.

'What's burning?' Then they all saw the curl of smoke creeping under the door.

Running to the door, Miss Tree opened it. Smoke billowed into the room from the landing. She slammed the door quickly.

'Well!' whispered Cleo to Bartle. 'Your rats have gone and done it now! They've chewed right through the wires – and set the house on fire!'

16

'Good boy, Hogarth!' exclaimed Kelly. 'You're doing brilliantly. Don't give up!'

They'd set off at the first hint of daybreak. Granpa, Dad and Joe sat squashed up together in the front of Dad's van, with Kelly and Hogarth in the back among the paint pots. They'd driven slowly along the deserted lanes around Acrefield for the last half-hour. To Joe, it felt like days. They must have gone *miles*, without seeing a jeep anywhere.

Then, just as he was starting to despair, Hogarth began to wriggle and bark.

'Stop!' cried Kelly. 'He knows where we are – let him out!'

Dad slowed down. Tumbling out of the van, Hogarth waddled energetically down a narrow, wooded lane. The van followed at a crawl.

Granpa sat quietly, his hands tightly clasped.

'Cleo,' he murmured.

Joe wished he could reassure him. He wished he could reassure himself. Megamouse, he thought. Where are you?

Hogarth halted, whining, at a rusty gate. Joe

scrambled out of the van to investigate. At the far end of a rutted drive he glimpsed a silver shape amongst the trees.

'The jeep! We've found it, Dad!'

'Good old Hogarth! I knew you could do it!' Kelly hugged the wheezing bulldog. But Joe sniffed.

'Dad? I can smell smoke!'

'Bonfire, maybe?' Dad suggested.

Joe bit his lip. It was too early for a bonfire. And if it was Miss Tree's fire – *what was she burning*? Panicking, he yanked at the gate, and raced up the drive.

As the cottage came into sight, Joe stopped in horror. Thick black smoke was pouring from a broken lower window. 'It's on fire!'

Dad grabbed at his coat.

'Wait, Joe! Stay well back! I'll go and look.'

As Dad stepped forward, Miss Tree appeared at an upper window, tugging at the catch. The window opened halfway – then stuck. Miss Tree put her head out and yelled at them.

'Get me down from here!'

'Where's Megamouse?' Joe yelled back.

'Here! You can have it – if you get me out of here!' she cried. She waved at him, and Joe saw something in her hand. Megamouse!

'Help me get the ladders,' said Dad. They ran to the van and hauled the ladders from its roof.

'Pa? Ring the fire service on my mobile,' called Dad.

'I'll do it!' cried Kelly. Dad carried the ladders over to the cottage and rested them against the wall. Granpa hobbled painfully behind on his crutches, and put a hand on Dad's arm.

'I don't want you going up there, son!'

'Don't worry, Pa!' said Dad cheerfully. 'I go up ladders all the time!'

'Not up blazing houses!' Granpa's voice trembled.

'It's not blazing, only smoking. But keep the children well back.'

Granpa seemed fixed to the spot. Joe pulled him back, and held his hand while they watched Dad climb nimbly up the ladder. Dad reached the window and wrenched at it until it opened fully. Then he helped Miss Tree climb over the sill. She descended the ladder at a run, still holding Megamouse in one hand.

'Whew!' she said as she reached the ground, then turned and laughed. 'That was exciting! I'm very grateful. Unfortunately – I'm not *that* grateful.'

And with a swift movement she swung Megamouse round by his tail and flung him through the broken downstairs window – straight back into the house. Joe saw the smoke swallow him up.

'No!' he cried in horror. As he dashed forward, Dad grabbed his jumper and hauled him back.

83

'You can't go in there! It's too dangerous.'

'But *Megamouse*!'

'Sorry, Joe.' Dad held Joe tight.

Miss Tree laughed. 'Well, goodbye, everyone! I must be off. So nice to meet you all.'

'Wait! You're under arrest!' thundered Granpa.

'For what? For stealing a computer mouse that talks? Who'll believe that?' She tossed her hair back. 'Your evidence is destroyed. Everything's burnt. Not that I care! It was all just a game anyway.'

'A game?'

'Of course!' she retorted. 'I made all the right moves! Why do you think I moved in next door? Why do you think I was so friendly? Why do you think I let Hogarth loose in your garden? That dog was my only mistake. If he wasn't so stupid, I would have won! *I* play to win.'

'You haven't won this time,' said Dad.

'Neither have you. So long, losers!' She strode to the jeep.

'Get her, Hogarth!' yelled Kelly. Hogarth galumphed up to Miss Tree and tried to bite her boots.

'We can't stop her,' said Granpa heavily. 'She's right. No evidence.'

'Get off me, you vile dog!' Miss Tree kicked Hogarth away, climbed into the jeep and started the engine. 'Escape!' she sang out, as she put her foot down. The jeep began to roll down the drive.

And Dad began to laugh. Joe, in his misery, looked up.

The jeep was juddering forward in tiny jerks. Joe saw that all four tyres were completely flat. Not just flat – shredded! Almost as if they'd been *chewed* . . .

'Drive carefully!' called Dad, as the jeep rattled down the drive, then stopped dead. Sirens wailed ahead, and a police car turned into the drive, followed by a fire engine. Flames began to dance in the cottage windows.

'Get right back!' commanded Dad. 'The roof could fall in at any minute.'

'But Megamouse!' wailed Joe. 'We've got to save him!'

'*No*,' said Dad firmly.

Joe stared at the cottage, his eyes stinging and blurring. The air was thick with smoke. He heard the flames' angry crackle and felt their fierce heat. Nothing could survive inside there now . . .

Then, by the front door, he saw a flicker of movement. A brown mouse and a white rat emerged from a drain, dripping wet, and tugging a tiny, round, grey, familiar shape . . .

'Megamouse?' Joe couldn't believe his eyes. Dragging him by his tail across the yard, they let go of their burden, drooping and exhausted.

'Megamouse!' Joe ran forward to pick him up.

'Cleo!' Granpa hobbled up and knelt beside him. The bedraggled white rat nuzzled his fingers wearily. The brown mouse scampered away into the bushes.

'Cleo!' said Granpa hoarsely. 'I thought I'd lost you!'

'Megamouse! You're safe now. It's me, Light Hand.' Joe cradled the mouse gently, trying to detect a twitch or tremble in the small grey body.

But there was none. Megamouse's shell was cracked and split – his tail was twisted and dirty. He was a piece of wire and plastic; nothing more.

'Granpa,' said Joe shakily. 'It's Megamouse all right . . . but I think he's dead.'

17

The living room was silent. Joe sat hunched in Granpa's chair; Cleo perched tensely by the computer. Together, they watched Granpa at work.

Granpa held Megamouse in one hand. The other hand twirled a tiny screwdriver.

He had removed Megamouse's broken shell. He had cleaned him, and replaced his battery. Now he was carefully fitting a new plastic casing.

'Don't know if this'll work,' he grunted.

Joe said nothing.

'Not really alive, you know,' said Granpa. 'Probably just a programming fault. Mice don't talk.'

Joe still said nothing.

'All the same – clever of you to discover it,' said Granpa. Joe was silent.

Granpa put Megamouse down.

'Sorry if I was rude to you, Joe,' he said gruffly. 'Doesn't mean I don't like you. Because I – er – hrmph. I do.'

'I like you too,' said Joe. He said it to be polite, and then realised it was true. He liked the deep growl of Granpa's voice, and his gentle hands stroking Cleo. And Granpa had surprised him by thanking all the firemen very politely after they'd doused the blazing cottage. Then he'd shaken hands with Dad, and even mumbled something about 'A brave lad, son,' with tears in his eyes.

'Sometimes you're nice,' said Joe.

Granpa made a noise between a snort and a laugh.

'Glad to hear it! So are you, sometimes.'

He gave the screwdriver a final, tiny twist and put it down.

'Finished,' he said. 'Looks better, doesn't he?' He held out Megamouse.

'*Looks* better,' Joe agreed with a sigh.

'He'd short-circuited,' explained Granpa. 'Full of water. The firemen said they'd never seen anything like it – fire and flood in the same house. Goodness knows how it happened. But the flood saved Megamouse's bacon – and Cleo's.' He gave Cleo an affectionate pat. 'Well, here goes. Let's try him out!'

Joe's fingers felt shaky as he plugged Megamouse in. He didn't think he could bear it if Megamouse didn't work . . . or, worse, had become just an ordinary mouse that couldn't talk . . .

Cleo sat up alertly as Joe typed:

'HALLO, MEGAMOUSE.'

The wait seemed endless. Then, at last, words began to appear on the screen.

'GREETING, LIGHT HAND.'

'Good heavens,' said Granpa faintly. He reached across the keyboard and typed in,

'AND HIS GRANPA.'

'GREETING, ANCIENT RELATIVE,' Megamouse replied.

'Hrmph!' said Granpa.

Joe grinned. 'HOW ARE YOU GOING?' he asked.

'ON MY LITTLE WHEEL.'

'It's talking gibberish,' said Granpa. 'Ancient, indeed!'

'WHAT HAPPENED?' Joe asked Megamouse.

'OUTSIDE WAS A VERY HARD GAME. *ROADHOG RACERS* WOULD NOT PLAY. ALL FUNCTIONS SHUT DOWN.'

'I don't believe it!' murmured Granpa.

'HOW DO YOU FEEL NOW?'

'I FEEL MOUSE MAT. NICE AND SOFT. I DO NOT LIKE PLAYING OUTSIDE.'

Megamouse rolled around his mat. His wheel squeaked faintly, and Cleo pricked up her ears and squeaked back.

'Hark at them!' said Granpa. 'You'd think they were talking to each other!'

'Maybe they are,' said Joe. 'After all, it was Cleo who rescued Megamouse – she must have followed him on purpose.'

'Hrmph!' said Granpa thoughtfully. 'Of course, I've always known she's a very intelligent rat. And

I wouldn't like to think she'd run away just because she wasn't happy.'

Joe bit his lip. He tapped in:

'MEGAMOUSE – WHY DID YOU RUN AWAY?' He already knew the answer that would appear on screen.

'ME BAD MOUSE.'

'NO!' answered Joe. 'GOOD MOUSE!'

'GOOD MOUSE?'

'VERY GOOD MOUSE! BEST MOUSE EVER!'

'GOOD GOOD GOOD!' Megamouse did a little twirl on the mouse mat. 'I HAVE LOTS OF NICE NEW NUMBERS,' he announced. 'YOU LIKE NEW NUMBERS?' Figures began to flood on to the screen.

Granpa stared in amazement. 'What on earth . . .? Good heavens! These files belong to some of the top computer companies!'

'WHERE DID YOU FIND THESE?' he asked.

'NAUGHTY COMPUTER OF COLD HAND.'

'Miss Tree!' exclaimed Joe.

'Stolen,' said Granpa. 'Well, her computer may have gone up in smoke – but we've got something to show the police now!'

'He's a clever mouse,' said Joe proudly.

Granpa cleared his throat. 'Hrmph. If I called you stupid, Joe, I was wrong. This Megamouse is the most interesting thing I've seen in years. Unique, in fact – and it was you who brought him to life!'

'I don't know how,' admitted Joe.

'Maybe we can find out. I'll look forward to testing him!'

'Testing? You won't hurt him, will you?' asked Joe anxiously.

'No. Just talk to him,' said Granpa gravely. 'In fact, I think you might be better at it than me. Maybe we could do it together.'

'You won't send him away?'

'When Cleo's so fond of him?' said Granpa. 'No, I'd rather keep him. Even if he does talk gibberish about *Roadhog Racers*. Is that a game you play with Kelly?'

'That's right. Would you like to play it, Granpa?' asked Joe tentatively. 'Or I could show you *Martian Warlord*. That's really cool!'

'You'd rather play with Kelly, I expect.'

'No, I wouldn't! Anyway, she's taken Hogarth to obedience class this evening. I think he'll keep her busy for a while.'

Granpa sniffed. 'I suppose I could play you for once, then,' he declared. 'These games can't be too difficult – not for someone who's worked with computers all their life. Don't be surprised if I win.'

'Winning's not everything, you know,' said Joe. He didn't care about being champion this time. He ıdn't really mind if he won or lost, so long as he had Megamouse – and Granpa – to play with.

'Just load it up,' commanded Granpa. 'I'll show you how it's done!'

Joe felt Megamouse give the faintest twitch beneath his hand.

'I wouldn't be so sure of that,' he said, and grinned. 'Ready, Megamouse? Ready, Granpa? Watch out, Martian Warlord – here we come!'